67

Famous 5 On the Case

LOOK OUT FOR THE WHOLE SERIES!

Case Files 1 & 2: The Case of the Fudgie Fry Pirates & The Case of the Plant that Could Eat Your House

Case Files 3 & 4: The Case of the Impolite Snarly Thing & The Case of the Sticks and Their Tricks

Case Files 5 & 6: The Case of the Plot to Pull the Plug & The Case of the Thief Who Drinks from the Toilet

Case Files 7 & 8: The Case of the Hot-Air Ba-Boom! & The Case of the Stinky Smell

Case Files 9 & 10: The Case of the Defective Detective & The Case of Allie's Really Very Bad Singing

D1160803

Case Files 11 & 12: The Case of the Medieval Meathead & The Case of the Messy Mucked Up Masterpiece

Case Files 13 & 14: The Case of the Guy Who Makes You Act Like a Chicken & The Case of the Felon with Frosty Fingers

Case Files 15 & 16: The Case of the Bogus Banknotes & The Case of Eight Arms and No Fingerprints

Case Files 17 & 18: The Case of the Flowers That Make Your Body All Wobbly & The Case of the Guy Who Looks Pretty Good for a 2000 Year-Old

Case Files 19 & 20: The Case of the Gobbling Goop & The Case of the Surfer Dude Who's Truly Rude

Case Files 21 & 22: The Case of the Cactus, the Coot, and the Cowboy Boot & The Case of the Seal Who Gets All Up In Your Face

Case Files 23 & 24: The Case of the Snow, the Glow, and the Oh, No! & The Case of the Fish That Flew the Coop

FAMOUS 5 ON THE CASE

THE CASE OF THE SEAL WHO GETS ALL UP IN YOUR FACE

Hodder Children's Books

A division of Hachette Children's Books

Special thanks to Lucy Courtenay and Artful Doodlers

Copyright © 2009 Chorion Rights Limited, a Chorion company

First published in Great Britain in 2009 by Hodder Children's Books

3

All rights reserved. Apart from any use permitted under UK copyright law, this publication may only be reproduced, stored or transmitted, in any form, or by any means with prior permission in writing from the publishers or in the case of reprographic production in accordance with the terms of licences issued by the Copyright Licensing Agency and may not be otherwise circulated in any form of binding or cover other than that in which it is published and without a similar condition being imposed on the subsequent purchaser.

All characters in this publication are fictitious and any resemblance to real persons, living or dead, is purely coincidental.

A Catalogue record for this book is available from the British Library

ISBN 978 0 340 98117 7

Typeset in Weiss by Avon DataSet Ltd, Bidford on Avon, Warwickshire

Printed and bound in Great Britain by Clays Ltd, St Ives plc

The paper and board used in this paperback by Hodder Children's Books are natural recyclable products made from wood grown in sustainable forests. The manufacturing processes conform to the environmental regulations of the country of origin.

Hodder Children's Books
a division of Hachette Children's Books
338 Euston Road, London NW1 3BH
An Hachette UK Company
www.hachette.co.uk

The Famous Five® and Enid Blyton® © Chorion Rights Limited. All rights reserved.

Chapter One

It was a perfect warm Californian evening.

The moon shone down on Malibu beach, illuminating the white sand and throwing long black shadows around the beach houses. Which suited a masked figure who was digging in the garden of the house where the Kirrins were staying with their American cousin, Allie.

Despite the helpful shadows, the masked figure couldn't help checking if he was being watched. What he was doing was highly illegal. If he had known that even at that moment, the Kirrins – plus Jo's dog Timmy – were heading back to the house after an evening out, he would have left a whole lot quicker. But as it was, he kept digging.

"What a great restaurant," said Max, happily stroking his stomach as he and the others strolled over the sand, approaching the beach house from the other side. "That's the best lobster I've ever had." He scratched head, ruffling his thick blond hair. "Then again it's the *only* lobster I've ever had, but still . . ."

Dylan burped, misting up his glasses a little. "I ate so much I'm starting to mutate," he said. "I'm turning into . . ." He waggled his fingers at the others. He'd stuck remnants of lobster claws and tails on his fingertips. ". . . Lobster Man!" he laughed, pinching together the claws on his thumbs and forefingers. "Woooooo!"

"Doesn't sound like a very good superhero," Jo said bluntly. She enjoyed popping Dylan's absurd bubbles every now and then. She was a practical sort of girl.

Dylan grinned. "I'm better when I team up with Jacket Potato Man."

Chatting and laughing, the cousins arrived at the patio on the beach-side of the house. The harbour seal who had taken to living in the patio fountain popped its whiskery head out of the water and barked a friendly greeting.

"Hiya, Oliver!" Allie said, waving a food bag at the seal. "We brought you a doggie bag. Or, in your case, an eccentric harbour seal bag. Guess what – it's fish!"

The seal barked with excitement as Allie removed a fish from the bag and tossed it into the fountain.

Feeling left out, Timmy whined and raised his handsome tan eyebrows at Jo. Smiling, Jo reached into her bag.

"And here's your bone, Timmy," she said, handing it over.

Oliver the seal wriggled out of the fountain as Timmy sank his teeth into his snack. He flopped energetically down to the edge of the water, which was tipped with silver light from the moon. Lifting his head from his bone, Timmy woofed at the seal, as if to say goodbye.

"Timmy," Dylan reassured him, "Oliver goes to the edge of the ocean every night. I think he washes his flippers off or something. But he always comes back."

They turned to watch Oliver wade a few metres into the water. The seal turned and barked at the Kirrins, before diving under the waves. They waited for him to surface and return to the beach house. But nothing happened.

"Ahh," said Dylan, frowning. "Looks like I'm wrong."

"That's it?" said Jo, feeling disappointed. "He just *left*?"

Max shrugged. "I suppose he likes the ocean again," he said sadly.

"I hope he stays in touch," said Allie. She

grinned. "Maybe he's got a *shell*-phone. Get it?"

"Not bad, Allie," Dylan admitted as Allie whooped and slapped her thighs. "I mean, not exactly earth-shaking . . ."

There was a booming sound under their feet. The earth quivered, making them reach for something to hold on to.

"And once again," Dylan admitted in faint surprise, "I'm wrong."

The ground was still shaking.

"It's an earthquake – get under the patio table!" Allie shouted.

The Five ducked under the table and put their arms over their heads. Would the whole building collapse around them?

At the back of the house, the masked figure stopped digging for a moment, assessing the strength of the tremor. Unconcerned, he returned to his task.

Chapter Two

Slowly, the earthquake subsided. Jo raised her head and peered out from underneath the table.

"I know California is prone to earthquakes, but that was the third in three days," she said, slowly getting to her feet. "I've got to say – I'm not warming to them."

"They freak me out," Max said in a shaky voice. "Plus, here you occasionally have brush fires, the odd mudslide . . . Let's stay under here for protection," he added, wriggling further under the table.

Dylan had stood up. Now he folded his arms and stared down at Max. "Not the *best* way to spend our holiday," he pointed out. "Maybe you should just put together an emergency kit."

Max raised his head. "That's a good idea," he said with relief and a little excitement. "It's what 'Lobster Man' would do."

Motivated by the idea of a practical project, Max scrambled out from underneath the table and joined the others inside. He grabbed his rucksack from the corner of the kitchen.

"You'll need bottled water," Jo began, pulling a bottle from the fridge and tossing it towards Max.

"Good, good – don't want to get thirsty," Max agreed. He stuffed the bottle into his rucksack. "And energy bars."

"What about crossword puzzles?" Dylan suggested as Max tucked some energy bars into the various pockets on his rucksack. "You don't want to get bored during a disaster . . ."

Max failed to notice the teasing note in Dylan's voice. He picked up some crossword puzzle books and stowed them in his bag. Then he headed for the cabinet near the window that overlooked the back garden. "And I like to watch DVDs when I do crosswords," he told the others over his shoulder. "Helps me think . . ."

Max's sentence trailed away as he saw the masked figure digging in the garden. He knocked on the window. "Hey!" he shouted through the glass. "What are you doing?"

Startled, the masked figure dropped his spade and started to run.

"He's heading round the house!" Max shouted, sprinting for the patio doors. "A man . . . with a . . . thing!"

"There's a man with a *thing*?" Dylan said. "Don't let him get away!"

The others ran out on to the beach after Max. Clutching his thing – a soil sample – the masked figure raced on ahead of them towards an area dotted with several beach volleyball courts. He ducked under the nets. Then he ran on to where a low chain-link fence surrounded a beach-side go-kart track. Slipping and sliding in the sand, the Five fought past the volleyball nets and leaped over the fence after him.

Several go-karts were parked on the small, wiggly karting track. The figure hopped into one of them and started it up. As the go-kart pulled away, Timmy ran in front of the wheels, barking madly. The masked driver forced the wheel left and right. No matter what he did, Timmy kept darting into his path.

The Kirrins found four go-karts of their own. Quickly, they pulled on helmets and seat-belts.

"Gentlemen, start your engines!" Dylan shouted, getting a little over-excited.

There was a roar of engines as the cousins started up their karts. The masked figure was now backing his kart away from Timmy and driving off in the opposite direction. The Kirrins pulled on the wheels of their karts and skidded after him.

Jo was good at speed. She put on an extra burst, and managed to come alongside the masked driver. Nudging at his kart, she forced him off the track – straight towards a huge pile of tyres.

"Woahhhhhhh!"

The figure flung his arms over his head and prepared to crash. Instead, the kart ploughed straight through the tyres, off the track site and out on to the coast road.

Tyres flew everywhere. As they bounced and

crashed down on the track, the Kirrins were forced to swerve and stop to avoid any nasty crashes.

The intruder had got away.

Chapter Three

The Five headed disconsolately back to the beach house. They hated it when villains escaped. Moving round to the back of the house, they studied the hole where the intruder had been digging before Max had disturbed him.

"If he was digging for clams, he was much too far from the ocean," said Dylan, poking at the hole with one toe. "And anyway, I don't really like clams."

"On the plus side, he unearthed some great rocks for my Emergency Kit," Max said. He picked up a couple of sizeable boulders. "In case I need to weigh down a tarpaulin or keep away a badger," he explained as the others frowned in confusion.

"There are no badgers around here," Allie pointed out.

"Good," Max said with relief. "One less thing to worry about."

Dylan pointed across the garden. "You know, Max," he said, "that sundial could come in handy in a power failure."

Once again, Max totally failed to pick up the sarcasm in Dylan's voice. "You're right!" he gasped, starting off in the direction of the sundial. "Someone give me a hand with it."

As Max tried to prise the decorative sundial out of the garden, the others watched him pityingly. Timmy meanwhile was sniffing at a tool left on the ground nearby.

"Look what Timmy found!" Jo said. Turning away from Max and his entertainment value, she headed back to the hole in order to pick up the tool and study it. "It looks like the tool my geology teacher uses to take soil samples."

"What's that number on it?" Allie asked, coming over as well.

Stamped into the handle was a series of letters

and numbers. *1256722NDSTLA.*

Taking the tool into the house, Jo laid it on the kitchen table. Max had given up on the sundial, and was now rummaging through the pots and pans in the kitchen cupboards.

"1256722NDSTLA," said Jo thoughtfully. She traced the marking with one finger. "Not much information to go on. It's not like we can trace it from just a serial number."

"Hey, Allie, where do you keep your towels?" Max asked. "I need them for my Emergency Kit."

"Don't forget the good china," Dylan advised as Max went off to hunt in the bathroom. "We don't want to live like animals."

"Towels are in the drawer, under the address-book!" Allie called after Max. She swung back to Jo as a thought struck her. "Wait a minute – 1256722NDSTLA," she said in excitement. "That could be an address. 12567 Twenty-Second Street, Los Angeles."

Dylan reached for his laptop. "I'll check it out online."

Max brought a selection of towels back into the

kitchen. He set them down beside his accumulated kitchenware.

"OK," he announced. "I've got saucepans, linens, salt and pepper. I guess a cookbook couldn't hurt . . ." Grabbing a book off the counter, he rifled through it for a moment. "Hmm," he said, momentarily diverted. "Bouillabaisse . . ."

"Got it," Dylan said, pushing back from his laptop. "12567 22nd Street is in Santa Monica. 'Don Jackson Geological Services'."

Jo held up the digging implement. "I think Don Jackson might be missing a tool," she said. "Let's take it back to him tomorrow."

Max looked up from his cookbook. "Allie," he began, "I'm going to need some garlic and some saffron . . ." He frowned at the enormous pile of items on the table in front of him. ". . . and a *much* bigger rucksack," he added.

The Five headed over to Santa Monica, in LA, the following morning. With Max wheeling an ungainly emergency suitcase along the pavement, the cousins were finding it hard to keep together.

"There it is," said Jo at last, pointing at a small shop front.

12567 Twenty-Second Street looked deserted and abandoned. One or two surly-looking workers were carrying shelves and assorted office equipment out of the shop.

"And it looks like it's gone out of business," said Dylan. He was good at pointing out the obvious stuff.

Allie clapped her hands girlishly. "Ooh, I hope a frozen-yoghurt-nail-salon-psychic-reader-shoe-boutique moves in!" she said. "We need more of those."

They went inside, and Jo approached a workman silently dismantling a bookcase. Wiping away a cobweb and brushing a little dust nonchalantly off one of the shelves, Jo cleared her throat.

"Has the geological business moved out?"

The workman ignored her.

"Any idea where to?" Jo pressed hopefully.

The workman turned his back on her and carried the bookcase outside.

"Thanks," said Jo sarcastically to his departing back. "You've been very helpful."

Dylan moved to the back of the shop. There, he found a life-sized cardboard cut-out of a paunchy, middle-aged man with teeth that were too white and a tan that was too orange. The cut-out's hand held a small container of promotional DVDs.

"Hmm," said Dylan, studying the DVDs. "Why would they leave *this* behind? 'Free Promotional DVD – Take One'." He glanced back at the others. "Maybe we can learn something about the company from it," he suggested, tucking a DVD into his pocket. "Plus, it's free, which is my favourite price!"

Max had finally appeared in the shop doorway. He was panting, and seemed pleased to stop pulling his suitcase for a while. "I've got a portable DVD player in the Emergency Kit," he said, bending down to the suitcase and pulling out a few items. "Food dehydrator, sock puppet, life raft . . ."

He put the raft down on the floor and continued hunting. With a loud "SSSSSSS!" the raft began to swell.

"Oops," said Max, looking round. "Raft's inflating."

He tried to sit on it. Despite this, the raft inflated to its full size. It took up most of the shop floor.

"Erm," Max said. "Maybe we should watch the DVD at home . . ."

He picked up the raft and tried to squeeze it out of the door, but it was too large. Timmy bit it helpfully and it deflated with a *pffft* sound.

"Thanks, Timmy," said Dylan, climbing over the wreckage to join the others outside. "Max," he advised, "maybe you should think about a wooden lifeboat . . ."

Chapter Four

Back at the beach house, the Five clustered behind Dylan as he loaded the DVD into his laptop.

"All right," Dylan said, flexing his fingers and sitting back while the laptop whirred. "Let's see what we can learn about 'Don Jackson Geological Services'."

The DVD scrolled through a few credits. The Five saw the man from the cardboard cut-out pop on to the screen. He wore a safari jacket and suit trousers, and a badly fitting curly toupée sat on his balding head. He appeared to be standing in some kind of meadow as he beamed at the camera.

"Hi!"

The Five winced at the bright combination of teeth and tan.

"I'm Chase Novak, star of the 1978 action series *Acapulco Station*," he continued. "You probably remember my catchphrase . . ."

Chase Novak struck a dramatic pose and pointed. Everyone waited expectantly.

"Look out!" said Chase.

"That's a good catchphrase," said Dylan, nodding. "Very flexible."

Chase Novak had resumed his normal position. "But I'm not chasing bad guys any more," he continued. "I'm here on my chinchilla ranch in Malibu."

Allie squinted at the top of Chase Novak's head. "Is that a toupée, or did one of his chinchillas climb on to his head?" she asked.

"When I needed a flood channel dug here on the ranch, I knew who to call," said Chase jovially. "Don Jackson Geological Services!"

A second man joined Chase on the screen. This guy was short and stocky, and looked very uncomfortable in front of the camera. He shook

Chase Novak's hand woodenly.

"Whether you need a sewer system installed, or a soil sample analysed, Don Jackson's the man to call," said Chase Novak, squeezing Don Jackson's hand tightly. "Ya . . . 'dig'?"

The Five couldn't tell if Don Jackson was wincing because of the dreadful pun, or because Chase Novak had him so firmly by the hand.

"If Chase Novak once had his own TV series and now he's doing sewer ads, he's *definitely* fallen on hard times," Dylan observed.

"I'd say he's hit rock bottom," Jo agreed. "But that DVD doesn't tell us much."

Dylan shrugged. "Tells us Chase Novak lives here in Malibu." He shot a mischievous look at Max. "And he worries about floods, Max."

Max looked horrified. "*Floods*! I have to be prepared for floods, too!?" he said, sounding faint. "I need sandbags! Hmm, where can I find sand . . . ?"

The faint whoosh of the ocean could be heard through the patio doors.

"Ah," Max said after a minute. "Outside!"

The others shook their heads in despair as Max looked through the kitchen drawers to find a couple of plastic bin bags, then hurried through the patio doors.

There was enough sand on Malibu beach to shore up the whole of Los Angeles. Feeling reassured, Max started filling his first plastic bag. Then he heard someone shouting out in the ocean.

"Hey, help! C'mon – cut it out!"

Max squinted, but couldn't make out much more than a pair of thrashing arms. Dropping his bag, he dashed back to the house. He grabbed a pair of binoculars from the patio table, and trained them out to sea.

"Someone's in trouble out in the water!" he shouted back into the house. The others came running.

A familiar-looking man was struggling in the water about a hundred metres offshore. Even at this distance, the gleam from his teeth and the glow from his tan was unmistakable. It was Chase Novak.

Max adjusted the binoculars. Chase looked as if he was having trouble with a circling dolphin – and a weird seal that Max knew all too well.

Oliver barked and slapped Chase playfully round the cheeks. The fat man looked like he was struggling. The Kirrins and Timmy ran down the beach, grabbed a set of boogie-boards and plunged into the water.

"Hey," said Dylan, "Chase Novak's got bigger problems than doing sewer ads – he needs to learn how to swim!"

Chase thrashed about helplessly. The kids swam as fast as they could, but the fat man was sinking . . .

Chapter Five

As the Five swam out to help the struggling TV star, they saw Chase Novak trying to grab on to a capsized inflatable boat. He'd clearly fallen out – or been pushed. The dolphin was still circling, doing its best to push the boat out of the actor's reach.

"Hang on, sir!" Allie yelled, paddling her boogie-board as hard as she could. "And don't panic – you have an otter on your head!"

"That's his wig," Jo said out of the corner of her mouth.

Allie blushed. "Oh. Oops," she muttered. "Never mind." And she concentrated on paddling for a bit.

Dylan had reached the inflatable boat. He

flipped it the right way up. Looking relieved, Chase Novak tried to pull his large bottom out of the water and into the boat. But Oliver the seal was having none of it. Even as Chase set his knee on the side of the inflatable for one last push, Oliver sank his teeth into the rubber. There was a nasty *pffft* sound, rather like the noise Max's raft had made in the deserted shop on Twenty-Second Street.

"Oliver!" Max shouted as the boat deflated, tipping Chase Novak back into the sea. "Leave this man alone!"

Oliver barked once, and swam away. Max turned to the damaged boat. It was almost under water already. "That's it," he said, shaking his head. "I'm getting a *metal* lifeboat for my Emergency Kit."

"You might want to get a Lifesaving Certificate while you're at it . . ." said Jo. She had hopped off her boogie-board and was trying to grab Chase Novak before he sank beneath the waves. As she pulled his head above water, the actor coughed up a small fish.

Expertly, Jo began swimming towards the shore, towing him along by the chin. The others followed, helping to keep the big man's nose above water until they reached the beach. Coughing and spluttering, Chase Novak crawled on to the sand and collapsed.

Two minutes later, the TV star had his mojo back.

"Thanks for helping me out of that little pickle, kids," he said, in the booming voice some adults save for talking to teenagers. "Coulda' swum ashore myself, but I cramped up . . ." He flexed his large and rather wobbly arms for effect before adding: " . . . from all the weights I've been lifting." He slapped his belly. His shirt buttons burst open and his flabby gut spilled over his waistband. "Yep," he said seriously. "Six pack."

Jo was the first to get everyone back on track.

"When you hired Don Jackson Geological Services for your flood channel, did you notice anything odd about any of the workers?" she asked.

Chase Novak looked confused. "Don Jackson?" Then his face cleared. "Oh, that commercial I did," he said. Sounding uncomfortable, he added: "Uh, I didn't know those people. That was just a quick gig I did for the cash."

Dylan nodded. "Cash is good," he said.

Chase Novak thrust back his shoulders. "I'm gonna make even more with my new project," he said. "An *Acapulco Station* reunion. I've been cruising the shoreline, scouting locations for it."

"How did you end up in the water?" Max asked.

"The seals and dolphins got rough with my boat," Chase explained. "Don't know what their deal is – they're supposed to be cute and cuddly."

Jo frowned. "That is weird," she said. "I thought Oliver and the other animals were back to normal." Ever since the Five had arrived in Malibu, the animals in the sea had been behaving strangely – until Oliver had returned to the ocean.

"Well, your beach is perfect for *Acapulco Station*," said Chase, waving his hand vaguely around the beach. "I'll get my crew here tomorrow. Big action scene. Explosions. Cool."

Max looked thrilled. "Brilliant!" he said. "I have an Emergency Kit if anything goes wrong."

"Swell . . ." said Chase. It looked like he had no idea what Max was talking about. He turned to Jo and Allie and switched on the charm. "Since you little ladies will be on hand, I think you might be perfect for a couple of small parts in the picture . . ." he said, and waggled his eyebrows meaningfully.

Jo and Allie gasped.

They were going to be film stars!

Chapter Six

The filming of *Acapulco Station: The Reunion* had begun bright and early. Down on the beach, Jo and Allie were dressed like a couple of Mexican peasants. Jo was holding a rope, which was attached to a cardboard donkey. Safely out of the way of all the action, Max and Dylan watched from the beach-house patio.

Out in the sea, Chase Novak was wading ashore. His wet-suit did a decent job of holding in his gut, and with the scuba on his back, he looked quite intrepid. As he reached the shore, he unzipped the wetsuit, revealing a tuxedo underneath.

The camera panned up the beach, following

Chase as he approached Allie and Jo.

"Hola, muchachas," said Chase, trying to keep up the intrepid thing. It didn't work so well in the tux. *"Dónde está la Casa Diablo?"*

Jo and Allie pointed up the beach.

"Gracias," said Chase. The TV star went into a defensive crouch, his eyes widening dramatically. *"Look out!"*

As he uttered his catchphrase and flung out one fist, he knocked over the cardboard donkey.

"Ooophhh," Chase grunted. He hopped to his feet and zigzagged up the beach, keeping low as he ran past assorted prop crates, cacti and rowing boats. The crates, cacti and boats all exploded once he was safely by. The cameraman looked bored, but followed as the action hero reached a parked dune buggy. Chase leaped into the driver's seat, tripping and falling heavily on to the seat.

"Ooophhh . . ."

Out of breath, Chase Novak squeezed his gut behind the buggy's steering wheel.

"And . . . cut!" he panted breathlessly. He mopped his forehead. "We'll have to do it again – I knocked over the donkey." Looking down at where the driving wheel was cutting into his belly, he added: "Somebody get me out of this sardine can, and set up for Take Eighteen."

Up on the beach-house patio, Dylan and Max shaded their eyes and watched as the sound guy tried to lever Chase out of the dune buggy, and the grip picked up the fallen crates and cacti.

"I love watching things explode," Max commented, "but eighteen takes seems a bit excessive."

"It's because Chase Novak keeps banging into the cardboard donkey," Dylan explained.

A bubbly African-American girl bounded

through the patio doors. It was Allie's best friend, Courtney.

"Hey, Dylan, Max – is my gallie-Allie doing her scene?" said Courtney brightly.

Dylan nodded. "She and Jo are out there now. Probably getting a headache from all the explosions."

Max slapped his forehead. "Explosions!" he gasped. "My Emergency Kit doesn't have anything, if – I mean *when* – space aliens attack!"

Courtney's eyes widened. "Space aliens are gonna attack?" she said. "They better not do it Thursday. I'm *totally* getting my hair done."

Max started feverishly making a new list. "I'll need cement to build a bunker. Then the bunker will need furnishing ..." He thought for a moment. "The loveseat and the rug!" And he dashed inside to start assembling furniture.

Courtney settled down beside Dylan. Even though they were some way from the action, there was still plenty to see. "Allie and Jo look mucho-riffic in their little outfits," she said, squinting at Allie and Jo in their ponchos. "Hey, why haven't I heard of this movie?"

"It's kind of a cheap-o, off-the-radar film," Dylan explained. "It has a cardboard donkey."

Courtney didn't look convinced. "I keep track of *every* movie," she said. "And every celebrity. Celebrities are national treasures. Except Chase Novak. He's a dingle."

Chase had waded out of the water and stripped off his wetsuit again.

"Hola, muchachas. Dónde está la Casa Diablo?"

Looking a little fed up now, Jo and Allie pointed.

"Gracias . . . Look out!"

This time, Chase missed the donkey. He lumbered up the beach and past the props.

"Hey," said Allie. "The props aren't exploding!"

Sure enough, the crates, cacti and boats stayed silent. Nevertheless, the girls both heard a series of BOOMs. The earth gave a rumble.

"So what's making all the noise?" said Jo nervously.

Chase stopped his run. "Cut! Cut!" he said irritably. "The pyrotechnics didn't work. Set it up again."

"Mr Novak," Allie called as Chase walked back down to his wetsuit and started wriggling into it again. "If the explosions didn't work, what was all that noise?"

"Well," said Chase, "the, uh, gonkulator didn't up-pilot with the hemi-fier, so, uh . . ." He dropped the wetsuit abruptly back on the sand and clapped his hands. "That's lunch, everybody! I'll be in my motor home."

As Novak strutted away up the beach, Allie and Jo heaved off their ponchos and headed thankfully towards the beach house.

"Hi, Jo-Jo. Heya, Allie-oop!" Courtney trilled.

"Hi Court!" Allie trilled back.

Trilling wasn't really Jo's bag. "Umm, heya too, Court . . . Court-ney," she said, giving up. Glancing back at the prop-strewn beach, she added: "I don't know much about movie making, but I think there's something fishy about this one."

Dylan already had his laptop open. "Well, for starters, it doesn't exist," he said, looking up from the screen. "I can't find a single website that mentions it."

The Five looked at each other. What was Chase Novak *really* up to?

"I say we pay a visit to Chase Novak's motor

home and get him to explain what's going on," said Jo at last.

"Could you help me finish up the food in the fridge first?" Max panted, coming out of the house with the entire refrigerator on a little wheelbarrow. "It's going to be unplugged till I get a generator for it."

"Come *on*, Max!" the others chorused, and grabbed him by the hand. They had some *serious* sleuthing to do!

Chapter Seven

Chase Novak had parked his motor home and truck at the edge of the road that ran along behind the beach house. The Five and Courtney approached the motor home cautiously, stopping to listen at the door.

"I'm Drake Hardcastle, Dr Diablo," they all heard Chase Novak say. "We can do this the easy way . . . or the *Hardcastle* way."

"Sounds like he's rehearsing his lines," Allie whispered to the others. She raised her hand and knocked on the door. "Mr Novak!" she called. "Mr Novak?"

"We can do this the easy way . . . or the

Hardcastle way," Chase Novak repeated.

Dylan sighed. "Let's do it the Hardcastle way . . ." he said, and opened the door.

A laptop sat on the floor inside. Chase's dialogue was repeating from it on a loop.

"Where did he go?" Max said in confusion, looking around the motor home.

"I don't know," said Jo. She peered out of the window. Chase Novak was coming down the road on the dune buggy. "But he's coming back."

The others looked at each other, alarmed. They were trespassing!

"Quick – hide under the motor home," Jo ordered.

Everyone scrambled for the door. Courtney looked reluctant.

"You guys like to get dirty more than I— *hoimp*!"

Jo grabbed Courtney before she could say anything else and dragged her down. They all lay quietly as Chase parked the buggy and walked towards them. The kids had a perfect view of his feet as they approached. His boots had little purple flowers stuck to them.

"Purple poppies!" Allie whispered as the actor

climbed into his motor home and closed the door behind him. "I know those – they only grow in shady areas in the hills round here."

"Is there anything like that nearby?" Max asked.

"There's a little grotto about half a mile from here," said Allie at once. She turned and smiled at her friend. "You coming, Courtney?"

Courtney looked up from examining a streak of mud on her trouser leg. "May as well," she sighed. "I can't get any dirtier . . ."

"Ugh, I was wrong," Courtney coughed half an hour later as Dylan knocked a shower of dust and pebbles all over her.

They were climbing up a steep, narrow footpath through the foothills that ran behind the beach. Behind Courtney, Max was trying to keep his Emergency Kit from pulling him back down the slope to the beach. He was failing.

"Oww," he yelled as the enormous trunk rolled back on its set of trolley wheels and whacked into him. "You think *you've* got trouble – my Emergency Kit's going to send me to the Emergency *Room*."

Jo was leading the way. She signalled to the

others to stop. "Hold on – I see something," she said.

The others joined her at the top – to see a huge encampment in the dip beyond. It was partially hidden by camouflage netting, and looked like an industrial drilling operation. Several enormous electricity generators, a huge drill positioned on a slant and a towering crane stood with their bases hidden among purple poppies. Everything bore a purple 'DJ' logo.

"When you say you see something," said Dylan, recovering first, "do you mean, something like a really cool bird's nest, or the secret drilling operation?"

"Look at the equipment – 'DJ'," Max gasped. "That's *got* to be Don Jackson."

They all saw the stocky, awkward-looking man from the promotional DVD step out from under a shade canopy with a large map in his hands.

"Yes," Dylan agreed. "There he is."

"And there's purple poppies all over – this must be where Mr Novak was," Allie added. "Which means he lied to us about not knowing Don Jackson."

They all lay low and watched Don Jackson approach one of the workers.

"Hey, Torvald – we've got to drill past the beach house by six o'clock. Novak's getting mad."

"That has to be our beach house," Allie said in excitement. Everything was starting to make sense.

"So they're drilling from here, underneath our house, out into the ocean," said Jo as she worked it out. "We can't hear it because of all the explosions on the film set."

"That's why no one's heard of the movie – it's just a distraction to cover the noise," Dylan put in.

Courtney looked pleased. "I knew it!" she said with pride. "My celebrity-sense hasn't failed me!"

"If they're drilling out into the sea, they must be drilling for oil," Dylan said. "There's oil all along the coast. Enough to make the finder really rich." He looked a little wistful.

"But isn't it illegal to drill for oil here?" Max protested. "It's just an environmental disaster waiting to happen."

Allie nodded. "That's why they're doing it from here," she said. "Where no one can see them. This whole operation shouldn't exist."

"Then we'll just have to stop it . . ." Jo said thoughtfully.

Down in the drilling camp ten minutes later, two workers wrestled the enormous drill bit into position. On cue, Timmy bounded out of the bushes. He barked playfully and wagged his tail.

"Hey, pooch, who are you?" said one of the workers, straightening up and smiling. "Wanna play fetch?"

Timmy darted to the nearby work-table and

grabbed the rolled-up map in his mouth.

"Hey," said the worker as the smile fell away from his face. "That mutt has the topographical map! We need that!"

Timmy romped between the workers as they tried to catch him. Then he started running away from the site. Exasperated, the workers ran after him.

Jo and Max stepped out of the same bushes and scampered over to one of the generators.

"Does this generator power the drill?" Jo asked Max anxiously.

"It won't after we ruin the carburettor . . ." said Max, turning to the assorted valves and buttons on the side of the generator.

Dylan was still in the bushes with Courtney and Allie. He was the first to spot another worker leaving a portable loo.

"Hey, he might spot Max and Jo," he said in alarm. He jumped to his feet, pulling Courtney with him. "Come on ..."

Dylan, Allie and Courtney raced down into the camp. They swerved towards a large stack of plastic pipes. Dylan grabbed a nearby spade and wedged it under the base of the stack. He, Allie and Courtney levered up the pipes, and sent them rolling everywhere.

Shouting with alarm, the workers scattered. Max and Jo ran for cover in the bushes.

"Good job, everyone," Jo panted as Allie, Dylan and Timmy ran over to join them. She glanced back. "Wait – where's Courtney?"

They all looked back at the camp. Courtney was lying on the ground, her foot tangled in a cable. As she tried to free herself, Don Jackson caught sight of her.

"Hey!" Jackson shouted, running over. "Who are you?"

"Aaah!" Courtney screamed. Jackson had taken one of her arms, and a worker had seized the other.

Allie gasped. *"They've got Courtney!"*

Chapter Eight

Helplessly, the Five watched from their hiding spot as Don Jackson dragged Courtney to a camp chair and forced her to sit down.

"What're you doing here, kid?" Jackson snarled. "Who told you we were here?"

Courtney rubbed her arm and looked injured. "I'm just looking for my dog," she said in an innocent voice. "He got off his leash."

The worker scratched his head. "There *was* a dog here before," he said.

Courtney nodded. "Yeah, he wandered off while I was looking for wild mustard for my 'Organic Foods' class at school," she said. "My teacher used to be a hippie."

"Wow, she's a gifted liar," said Dylan, impressed. "That's brilliant."

He caught the others frowning at him.

"Though, of course, morally wrong," he added hastily.

Don Jackson sounded sceptical. "There's no wild mustard around here."

The Kirrins winced. Courtney's brilliant lie wasn't holding up.

The generator seized up with a loud metallic grinding. As it stopped, black smoke belched out.

"Hey, boss," called one of the workers. "Something's happened to the generator."

Don Jackson paled. "All right, kid," he said at last, "I don't know who you are, but you're coming with me."

He dragged Courtney to a nearby Jeep, and shoved her into the seat. He jumped in beside her, clipped the seatbelts into place and pulled away from the camp. The Five watched as the Jeep rumbled away down the dirt road.

Back at the beach, Chase Novak was in a filthy mood.

"We're running crazy late," he complained to the cameraman. He adjusted his waistband. "This girdle is killing me." He scratched his head. His toupée wobbled. "And I've got sand under my hair," he finished in disgust.

Don Jackson strode round the corner, dragging Courtney with him.

"Who's this?" said Chase, perking up. "She one of my fans?"

"Looks like somebody sabotaged our generator," Don Jackson said grimly. "It's gonna be down all day."

"Did you do it?" Chase hissed at Courtney. "How much do you know?"

Courtney stared him down. "Umm," she drawled, "I know you're a lousy actor."

Chase Novak's eye started twitching. "I hate critics," he snarled, grabbing a piece of gaffer tape and putting it across Courtney's mouth. "Take her to the yacht," he ordered Don Jackson over his shoulder. "We'll find out what she knows later."

Don Jackson hustled Courtney down to the water's edge, where a small boat lay on the sand. As they climbed into the boat, the sound of cheerful chattering filtered down to Chase from the beach house.

"Hey, Mr Novak!" said Allie, waving as the Five came innocently out of the house. "How come the filming hasn't started back up?"

Chase Novak gathered his wits. "Er, we had some problems with notes from the studio," he said, glancing a little nervously at the dinghy. Jackson was waiting for him, trying to keep Courtney under control. "I've got to get back to my yacht, do some re-writes. See you kids later."

Chase headed for the dinghy. The Five watched as Don Jackson piloted the little boat out into the waves, towards a yacht lying at anchor a little way offshore.

Allie dropped her cheery tone of voice. "They're taking Courtney to his boat," she said.

The cousins folded their arms and stared out to sea.

"Then he's going to see us sooner than he thinks . . ." Allie murmured.

Chapter Nine

That evening, a full moon hung low in the sky. Chase's yacht bobbed on the still water, a black outline on the glowing sea.

Wearing life-jackets, the Five rowed quietly alongside the yacht in a lightweight metal boat. They tied up to the yacht's ladder, and silently signalled to each other to climb aboard.

Max went first. Well, strictly speaking, his Emergency Kit went first, as Max heaved and panted and shoved it up the ladder and down on to the deck. The others followed as patiently as they could.

Jo was the last to reach the top. The others were

on the deck at the back of the ship, examining some high-tech equipment: a computer screen and what looked like a loudspeaker on a long wire wrapped round a winch.

"This is sonar equipment," said Dylan, examining the screen and the loudspeaker. "They can hoist it over the side and do echo-locating."

Echo-location was a way of bouncing sound off objects to work out what and where they were. Dolphins used it to find fish. Bats too. (Bats looked for insects, not fish. Looking for fish in the air would be stupid.)

"So this is how they looked for the oil," Jo breathed, studying the equipment.

Allie shrugged. "They probably weren't looking for vinegar . . ." she quipped.

Max looked puzzled. "But the sonar noises in the water would drive the sea mammals crazy."

"That would explain why the dolphins were so aggressive," said Dylan, snapping his fingers as he realised. "And why Oliver was all . . ." he continued, slapping Max lightly around the face a few times.

"Yes, it would," said Max. He pushed Dylan's

hands away. "Though I don't think the slaps were that necessary."

"Maybe that's why the animals attacked Novak . . ." Allie said, working it out.

"We've *got* to let the Coastal Commission know about this," said Jo, starting back towards the ladder. "An oil spill would be a disaster for the environment."

"First," Allie reminded her cousin, "we've got to find Courtney and get her out of here."

Jo stopped. They all looked round the yacht, listening carefully for the sound of voices.

It didn't take long.

"We can do this the easy way . . . or the *Hardcastle* way," they heard Chase Novak growling.

The Five exchanged glances. They hurried down the deck towards the sound. It was coming from the pilot-deck. Creeping up the pilot-deck stairs with the others on his tail, Dylan peered through the windows. He gasped and half-covered his eyes.

"Oh, no – poor Courtney," he muttered, sounding horrified.

"What are they doing to her?" Allie said in alarm.

Dylan peeped over the top of his hands. "Making her watch an old episode of *Acapulco Station*!"

The others jostled up beside Dylan and peeped through the window as well.

Courtney was tied up and gagged in front of a TV set. The screen showed a younger Chase in a white linen suit, holding a hoodlum by the shirtfront in some seedy alley. Chase Novak and Don Jackson were nowhere to be seen. The Five realised that the voice they'd heard was coming from the TV.

They burst into the pilot-house. Courtney gasped with relief as Jo untied her and pulled the tape off her mouth.

"I'm so glad you're here," she panted. Tears came to her eyes. "That Chase guy is the worst actor I've ever seen."

"Then it's a good thing I've moved into oil exploration."

The Five whirled round. Chase Novak and Don Jackson were both standing in the pilot-house doorway, holding heavy spanners.

* * *

There was no point in fighting. The Five and Courtney allowed themselves to be led down on to the stern deck.

"So you've been cruising the coast searching for oil," accused Jo over her shoulder. "And you found some, offshore in front of our beach house."

"But you couldn't just set up a drilling platform in the ocean – it's illegal," Max continued.

Allie took over. "So you had to drill from *onshore*. From a hidden glade so you could stay secret."

"And you had to drill under our house to get to the oil," Dylan continued, patting the control panel that stood beside the winch they'd studied earlier.

"That's why you were digging in our yard – to get soil samples to see what you'd be drilling through," finished Max.

"You kids make good detectives," Chase snarled. "You could have written for *Acapulco Station*."

"*Timmy* could have written for *Acapulco Station*," Courtney said tartly.

Looking offended, Timmy gave a low growl. Jo patted him. "It's OK, Timmy – she was only joking," she soothed. "She didn't mean to insult you."

"But being smart isn't gonna do you any good," said Chase with a nasty smile. "We're gonna keep you on this boat and make sure you don't tell anybody about this."

"Then we'll extract the oil and get stinking rich before anyone knows what's happening," Don Jackson added, laughing.

Jo glared at the two villains. "You're right about the 'stinking' part," she snapped.

Dylan's hand was still on the winch control panel. He quietly flipped the switch. Novak and Jackson were so busy glaring back at Jo that they didn't notice the loudspeaker as it lowered quietly into the sea.

"Sorry about this, Oliver," Dylan muttered under his breath. "We have to bother you one more time . . ."

The loudspeaker – or transducer, to give it its proper name – began sending out loud sonar *pings*. The unpleasant sound rippled out under the water, passing several irritated dolphins and eventually reaching Oliver. At once, the seal sped over to a nearby humpback whale. He swam around the humpback until, at last, the enormous creature started following him.

Chase Novak and Don Jackson were in for a whale of a surprise.

Chapter Ten

Back on the yacht, Don Jackson had started tying Jo's hands.

"We'll keep them down in the bilge," said Chase Novak nastily. He was fed up with these snooping kids. "See how they like *that*."

The yacht gave a violent lurch. Novak, Jackson, Courtney and the Five grabbed hold of anything they could reach to prevent themselves being thrown overboard.

Out in the water, the most astonishing sight met their eyes. The huge humpback and a dozen dolphins were ramming the yacht's hull repeatedly. In the background, Oliver was leaping out of the waves and barking encouragement.

The kids hung on to the railings tightly as the whale rammed the yacht again. Everything shuddered. Novak and Jackson were thrown off-balance.

"Wooaahh!"

"Heyyyyy . . ."

Seizing her chance, Jo pushed Jackson over some of the deck equipment. He crashed helplessly to the ground. Timmy leaped on to Chase Novak with a growl and knocked him flat.

"Ooophhhh!"

"Ohhhhhh!"

Max crawled across the lurching deck. He pulled himself up by the ship-to-shore radio and leaned in to the microphone. "Mayday, mayday," he panted. "Boat in distress two miles off the Malibu coast, near Paradise Point." He looked over at the others. "That'll bring the Coastguard!"

Jo took charge. "Allie – start the engine when I give the signal," she ordered.

Allie and Courtney scampered up to the pilot-house. Jo and Dylan switched off the transducer and reeled it back up into the boat. Moving the cable until it was directly over the stern, they then lowered it back down.

When the transducer was in position, Jo waved at the pilot-house.

Courtney waved back. "Hi, Jo! This is fun!" she called happily. "Oh," she added after a couple of seconds, "I think that's the signal . . ."

Allie pushed the start button. The yacht's propellers started to spin, wrapping the transducer's steel cable around itself until it fouled and ground to a halt.

Chase Novak clambered unsteadily to his feet. So did Don Jackson. Growling softly, Timmy kept a close eye on them both.

"Sorry, Novak – this yacht isn't going anywhere," said Jo cheerfully.

"Then I guess *we'll* go," Chase said.

He and Jackson both raced across the deck and climbed into the inflatable dinghy, which hung over the side of the yacht.

"I'm not sticking around to explain things to the Coastguard," Chase continued.

He released the davits holding the dinghy in the air. It dropped like a stone, landing on the water.

Chase started up the outboard motor, and began to turn the dinghy's nose towards the shore.

At last, the big moment for Max's Emergency Kit had come. He dragged the kit to the edge of the boat as Jackson roared at Chase Novak to hurry. "I guess this qualifies as an emergency," he panted. "Good thing I have my Emergency Kit . . ."

He heaved the huge trunk over the side of the yacht. It plunged down into the dinghy – and kept right on going, ripping straight through the bottom of the rubber boat. The dinghy promptly sank, leaving Chase Novak and Don Jackson floundering in the water.

On cue, Oliver the seal surfaced. He slapped Chase smartly around the face.

"Owww!" wailed the villain.

He was well and truly washed up.

Back on the beach a little later, the kids watched as a sheriff led Chase and Jackson away in handcuffs. Sirens blinked on the roadside. TV crews were skulking in the background, their camera lights looking bright in the evening gloom.

The patio door to the beach house swung open, and Jo's parents appeared.

"Hello everyone," said George, waving enthusiastically. "We're home from the mildew conference! It was everything I hoped it would be!"

Ravi spotted Chase Novak as he was being helped into one of the police cars.

"Hey, it's Chase Novak!" he gasped in delight. "I finally saw a movie-star! Sure, he's in handcuffs, but so many are these days . . ."

Courtney looked sad that all the excitement was

over. "So you guys really go back to England tomorrow?" she asked.

"I'm afraid so," Jo said. She glanced wistfully up the beach. "And we still haven't ridden the rollercoaster on the pier. Or collected starfish in rockpools."

"Or gone para-sailing," Max added, "or ridden our bikes in Griffith Park."

"Then you know what I think?" Dylan announced, clapping his arms around his cousins' shoulders. "I think we're going to have a very busy night!"

And the cousins cheered and ran up the beach together.

Oliver the seal and a local dolphin poked their heads up out of the ocean to watch the Five go. Oliver barked, and the dolphin added a couple of whistles. Turning his head as he pelted after Jo, Timmy barked in reply.

"Bye, Oliver – thanks for your help!" Max shouted, turning round. "Now you guys have a nice, quiet ocean again," Allie added. "Unless like, whale burps are really loud." She frowned, looking a bit disgusted. "I never thought about it before . . ."

Jo stopped running as she realised she'd lost the others. "Um, Allie, Max . . . ?" she called. "Para-sailing?"

"Right!" Allie and Max replied promptly, and started running again.

Epilogue

Despite the illegal oil mining operation, the foothills that the Five had found the previous day had been very pretty. That was where they decided to shoot their final Californian Handy Hint.

It was Jo's turn behind the camera. Dylan took up position among some of the purple poppies, holding tightly to a small case.

"Sticky Situation Number Four Hundred and Ninety-One: You Need To Evacuate," said Jo.

Dylan cleared his throat. "It's important to have an Emergency Kit, in case you ever have to evacuate," he informed the camera. Kneeling on the ground, he put the case down. "That way," he continued as he unbuckled it, "in the middle of nowhere, you'll still have water, non-perishable food and an emergency blanket."

He flipped open the lid and pulled out some lipstick, a hairbrush and a cosmetics compact.

"Just make sure you don't grab Allie's make-up kit by mistake," he added, staring at the lipstick in surprise.

Allie appeared in Jo's line of vision now. She took the hairbrush from Dylan and started brushing her hair. "But if you do," she continued with a bright smile for the camera, "at least you'll look good."

FAMOUS 5 ON THE CASE

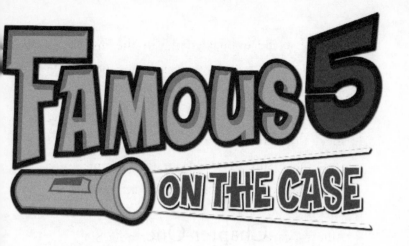

THE CASE OF THE FUDGIE FRY PIRATES

Read on for Chapter One
of the Famous 5's first Case File . . .

Hodder Children's Books

A division of Hachette Children's Books

Chapter One

A seven-metre sailboat sat on wooden supports outside the shed. Wearing grungy clothes, a toolbelt and a cap, Jo was in a suspended bosun's chair halfway up the boat's mast, polishing it with a cloth. Her elbow was starting to hurt.

"You've started, so you've got to finish," Jo told herself firmly, pushing her brown hair behind her ears.

She glanced down to where a large and very hairy dog was snoozing in the shade cast by the boat's hull. "You've got it right, Timmy," she sighed, wiping her forehead.

Timmy woofed gently and rolled on to his back.

"Be careful up there, Jo," warned Jo's mum George, who was potting something bushy in a terracotta tub down in the yard below. "If you fall, you'll crush my Devil's Moustache."

"Thanks for the concern, Mum," Jo said sarcastically. She turned back to the mast and rubbed it hard. "Shine!" she growled. "Shine more!"

She slapped the mast with her cloth in frustration.

"Whoa!"

Jo's sudden movement made her chair wobble. She dropped her polishing cloth and flailed her arms as she and the chair went spinning head over heels, getting tangled in the boat's ropes.

Timmy leaped to his feet and started barking fiercely. Jo grabbed the mast and used it to spin herself back in the other direction. She did a neat backflip out of her bonds and landed on the ground like a gymnast, missing the Devil's Moustache by a whisker.

"I'll get this shipshape before Max and Allie and Dylan get here if it kills me," Jo said. She slapped the boat, which promptly toppled over on top of her. "Which it just might do," she added in a muffled voice.

The honk of a taxi horn floated down from a nearby hilltop.

"Oh!" said Jo in excitement. "They're coming!"

She struggled to push the boat off her as the taxi trundled into view, pursued by a tall blond boy on a mountain bike pedalling for all he was worth.

"Attaboy, Timmy," Jo said, scrambling free as Timmy tugged her arm. "Oh, I hope everyone's ready to have some cool adventures! I've got a lot of things planned."

Her jumper caught on the boat and unravelled. George raised her eyebrows.

"What?" said Jo. "I can have adventures with half a jumper."

"Whoo!" shouted Max, pedalling like fury behind the taxi. There was no way he was going to let Allie and Dylan get to Jo's house first.

Swerving off the road, Max plunged down the side of a hill, jumped a fence and started slaloming through some startled cows. "'Scuse me!" he shouted. "Pardon me, ladies! Short cut!"

The hill suddenly got steeper. Max twisted his wheels and took off, straight through the middle of a hay cart. Coughing and trailing haystalks, he landed on the other side and continued on his downward plunge.

The taxi containing his cousins was almost at Jo's gate. Putting on a fresh burst of speed, Max twisted his handlebars one more time and leaped over another fence, landing in Jo's yard just as the taxi pulled up.

"Hey, Jo!" Max called, squealing his bike to a halt. "It's so great to be here!"

His front tyre hit an upturned rake lying in the middle of the yard. The tyre exploded and the bike stopped abruptly, causing Max to fly over the handlebars towards the boat and hit his head on the ship's bell.

Dong!!

"That's going to sting a while," said Max, rubbing his head woozily. "Hey, great boat, though! Really brilliant!"

Dylan kicked open the taxi door. He was holding a DVD camera in one hand, his dark hair flopping to one side.

"Max, bash into that boat again," he said. "I can sell the footage to 'World's Wackiest Wipe-Outs'.

Do you think you could bleed a bit?" he added seriously. "That'd really help me out."

Allie scrambled out of the taxi. "Hey Jo!" she said happily, her blond hair bouncing on her shoulders and her pretty skirt somehow totally uncreased. "Love your half-a-sweater! What a neat style! Hi, Aunt George!"

"Lovely to see you, dears!" George smiled, waving her potted plant. "I'll go and get lunch ready."

Allie eyed the plant. "Is that some kind of . . . salad, Aunt George?"

Enid Blyton™

THE
FAMOUS FIVE'S
SURVIVAL GUIDE

Packed with useful information on surviving outdoors and solving mysteries, here is the one mystery that the Famous Five never managed to solve. See if you can follow the trail to discover the location of the priceless Royal Dragon of Siam.

The perfect book for all fans of mystery, adventure and the Famous Five!

ISBN 9780340970836

Read the adventures of George and the original Famous Five in

Five On A Treasure Island
Five Go Adventuring Again
Five Run Away Together
Five Go To Smuggler's Top
Five Go Off In A Caravan
Five On Kirrin Island Again
Five Go Off To Camp
Five Get Into Trouble
Five Fall Into Adventure
Five On A Hike Together
Five Have A Wonderful Time
Five Go Down To The Sea
Five Go To Mystery Moor
Five Have Plenty Of Fun
Five On A Secret Trail
Five Go To Billycock Hill
Five Get Into A Fix
Five On Finniston Farm
Five Go To Demon's Rocks
Five Have A Mystery To Solve
Five Are Together Again

FAMOUS 5 ON THE CASE

LOOK OUT FOR THE WHOLE SERIES!

Case Files 1 & 2: The Case of the Fudgie Fry Pirates & The Case of the Plant that Could Eat Your House

Case Files 3 & 4: The Case of the Impolite Snarly Thing & The Case of the Sticks and Their Tricks

Case Files 5 & 6: The Case of the Plot to Pull the Plug & The Case of the Thief Who Drinks from the Toilet

Case Files 7 & 8: The Case of the Hot-Air Ba-Boom! & The Case of the Stinky Smell

Case Files 9 & 10: The Case of the Defective Detective & The Case of Allie's Really Very Bad Singing

Case Files 11 & 12: The Case of the Medieval Meathead & The Case of the Messy Mucked Up Masterpiece

Case Files 13 & 14: The Case of the Guy Who Makes You Act Like a Chicken & The Case of the Felon with Frosty Fingers

Case Files 15 & 16: The Case of the Bogus Banknotes & The Case of Eight Arms and No Fingerprints

Case Files 17 & 18: The Case of the Flowers That Make Your Body All Wobbly & The Case of the Guy Who Looks Pretty Good for a 2000 Year-Old

Case Files 19 & 20: The Case of the Gobbling Goop & The Case of the Surfer Dude Who's Truly Rude

Case Files 21 & 22: The Case of the Cactus, the Coot, and the Cowboy Boot & The Case of the Seal Who Gets All Up In Your Face

Case Files 23 & 24: The Case of the Snow, the Glow, and the Oh, No! & The Case of the Fish That Flew the Coop

FAMOUS 5 ON THE CASE

THE CASE OF THE CACTUS, THE COOT, AND THE COWBOY BOOT

Hodder Children's Books

A division of Hachette Children's Books

Special thanks to Lucy Courtenay and Artful Doodlers

Copyright © 2009 Chorion Rights Limited, a Chorion company

First published in Great Britain in 2009 by Hodder Children's Books

3

All rights reserved. Apart from any use permitted under UK copyright law, this publication may only be reproduced, stored or transmitted, in any form, or by any means with prior permission in writing from the publishers or in the case of reprographic production in accordance with the terms of licences issued by the Copyright Licensing Agency and may not be otherwise circulated in any form of binding or cover other than that in which it is published and without a similar condition being imposed on the subsequent purchaser.

All characters in this publication are fictitious and any resemblance to real persons, living or dead, is purely coincidental.

A Catalogue record for this book is available from the British Library

ISBN 978 0 340 98117 7

Typeset in Weiss by Avon DataSet Ltd,
Bidford on Avon, Warwickshire

Printed and bound in Great Britain by
Clays Ltd, St Ives plc

The paper and board used in this paperback by Hodder Children's Books are natural recyclable products made from wood grown in sustainable forests. The manufacturing processes conform to the environmental regulations of the country of origin.

Hodder Children's Books
a division of Hachette Children's Books
338 Euston Road, London NW1 3BH
An Hachette UK Company
www.hachette.co.uk

The Famous Five® and Enid Blyton® © Chorion Rights Limited.
All rights reserved.

Chapter One

The Old Wild West had come to life.

The Kirrin cousins, plus Jo's dog Timmy, stared round at the bank, the saloon, the horse trough and the old wooden verandas that lined the dusty old-fashioned street. If it hadn't been for the assorted rides, colourful stalls and the fact that the horses were made of plastic, they could have slipped back in time.

Allie shifted her backpack to a more comfortable spot. She tossed her blond hair over her shoulder, and leaned in to see what it said on the large, cheery-looking map in front of her.

"Welcome to Scrappy Flapjacks' Cowboy Town!"

she read. "No visit to Los Angeles is complete without it."

It was thanks to Allie that the Kirrins were in the States. Her parents had gone away, leaving Jo's family in charge of the cousins down at Allie's beach house in Malibu. They were making the most of their time in the California sun.

Max pushed his shaggy blond fringe out of his eyes and pointed at the map. "Can we ride the stagecoach?" he said in excitement. "YEEEE-HAAAAAGH!" He coughed a bit. "That actually hurts a little," he confessed sheepishly.

Dylan had found something far more interesting on the map. "We can pan for gold?" he gasped. His glasses started steaming up at the prospect of cash. "That's got my name all over it. Although I'd rather use a really big vacuum cleaner."

Allie turned to consult her third and final cousin. "What do *you* want to do, Jo?" she said.

There was no sign of Jo.

"Jo? . . ." Allie called, looking round in confusion. "Jo?"

Jo had wandered over to a game booth, where you had to shoot a little bow and arrow at balloons

to try and pop them. This was more her kind of thing than gold or stagecoach rides.

"I only have to pop three balloons?" Jo was checking with a craggy looking woman dressed in a US Cavalry outfit, who was in charge of the booth. "Why don't you just *give* me a prize?"

The woman handed Jo the bow and arrows. "Careful, girlie," she said in a patronising tone of voice, "it's not as easy as it—"

THWACK-THWACK-THWACK!

In quick succession, Jo fired the arrows and popped the balloons.

"—looks," the woman finished uncertainly. She shrugged, trying not to look impressed. "Oh, OK, what prize do you want?"

"I wanna horseshoe!" screeched a child, before Jo had a chance to choose something. He pointed his grubby little fingers at the prizes ranged round the booth. "I wanna tepee!"

As he pointed, he knocked over his cup of juice. The sticky purple drink spilled all over the booth's counter. Now his voice rose an octave.

"I spilled my juice," he roared, slapping his hands in the purple mess and sending it everywhere. "WAAAAGGHHHHH!"

"Hey, buckaroo," said the woman behind the booth, trying desperately to sound cheerful. "Only smiles at Scrappy Flapjacks'! This is a happy— you're getting grape juice everywhere, you pipsqueak!"

With a heavy sigh, she got a cloth and started cleaning up the mess. "Grab a prize, girlie," she told Jo over her shoulder.

Jo's cousins had caught up with her, and they all stared at the choice of prizes. There was a clown in a cowboy hat, a model covered-wagon, a tepee with

a clock in it and various soft toys that dangled from the booth's roof.

"So what are you going to take?" asked Allie, pressing in eagerly behind Jo. "The clown with a cowboy hat is nice."

Jo spotted a small ceramic cactus tucked in amongst the prizes. "Mum likes plants," she said, leaning over and taking the cactus. "She'll love getting this when she and Dad come back from Sequoia."

"Can we pan for gold now?" Dylan begged. "I hear it calling to me."

The cousins moved away, joking and laughing. The woman at the booth was still mopping up when a phone started ringing under the counter. She put down her cloth and picked up the phone.

"Hello? . . ." Suddenly her voice dropped down low. "Yeah, I got the component . . ." she said, glancing round to make sure no one was listening. "It's right here, hidden in a cactus . . ."

Still with the phone pressed to her ear, she peered over at the stack of prizes. A look of panic crossed her face. "Where is it?" she muttered. "Where'd it go?"

As she caught sight of Jo carrying the cactus away, her expression hardened.

"Er, little problem with the cactus," she said into the phone, watching as the cousins made their way across Cowboy Town towards the gold-panning area. "But don't worry – I know where it is . . ."

She hung up and watched as Jo put the cactus into her rucksack.

". . . and I'm going to get it back . . ." she said quietly to herself.

Chapter Two

The Five made it back to Allie's Malibu beach house later that afternoon. Chatting and laughing, they came in through the front door, their arms full of take-away food bags.

"You know what I love about Los Angeles?" said Max.

"The carefree lifestyle?" Allie guessed, frowning. "The glamour of Hollywood?"

Max waved his food bag happily. "Take-away tacos!"

They went on through the living room and out on to the patio. A fountain tinkled refreshingly in the afternoon sun. Sitting down at the patio table,

they unwrapped their food and started tucking in.

Dylan studied his food curiously, looking at it from all angles. "What did you say this is again?" he checked with Allie.

"A chimichanga," said Allie.

Dylan grinned. "Chimi-channnga!" he said, in a comedy Mexican accent.

Max laughed.

"I've got to warn you guys – this is authentic Mexican food," said Allie, unwrapping her portion and setting it down on a plate. "Some of the peppers are really hot."

Max shrugged, unimpressed. "I've had English mustard," he said. "That's hot."

"Chimi-*chaannnnga* –" Dylan repeated with gusto. He sank his teeth into his chimichanga and took an enormous bite. His eyes bugged out of his head. "Haagghhh-haghhh-haghhh . . ."

Max roared with laughter at the sight of Dylan choking and wheezing. "Little hot for you?" he hooted. He bit into his own food. If anything, his face went redder than Dylan's.

"Little more kick than mustard, hey, Max?" Jo said, amused.

"Whuuhhh . . . no!" said Max hoarsely, trying to bring the choking under control. "No – I love it!"

"Me too!" Dylan gasped, tears starting in his eyes as he forced a smile. "I wish it was hotter!"

Now the sweat started streaming down their faces. Max cracked first. "Water!" he croaked.

"Need water!" Dylan choked in agreement.

Dropping their food on the table, they scurried over to the large patio fountain and started scooping the water into their mouths. Timmy sniffed the chimichangas experimentally. His black nose wrinkled in alarm, and he backed away from the table.

Just then, they all heard a strange barking. Dylan lifted his head from the fountain and stared at Max in surprise. "Wow, Max – that pepper really messed up your voice," he said.

Max was staring at the visitor who had flopped on to the patio. It was the harbour seal that had followed him the last time he'd been surfing.

"It's not me," he said, pointing. "It's that seal who keeps beating me up."

The seal's friendly face seemed to grin at the Five. It started flopping rapidly towards Max,

before hopping into the fountain and sending a huge arc of water over everyone.

"Hey you . . ."

"Stop it . . ."

"Don't do that . . ."

"I'm all wet!"

Max mopped himself down. "He's crazy, I tell you!" he said, more than a little nervously. "He's dangerous!"

The seal propped itself up on its flippers and gave Max a whiskery, fish-flavoured kiss. Then it ducked back down into the fountain and started swimming around.

"He likes you!" Allie said in delight. It wasn't every day a cute seal made its way into her patio fountain.

"Then he *must* be crazy," said Jo, rolling her eyes. She looked at the seal. "Why are you in the fountain?" she asked. "Don't you want to go back in the ocean?"

As the Five listened to the seal's reply, a dark figure was climbing carefully into the house through a window next to the front door. The woman from the game booth at Scrappy Flapjacks'

had come to reclaim the ceramic cactus. Her face was covered by a ski mask, which she lifted to get her bearings, then replaced and started looking round the room.

Outside on the patio, the seal was now rubbing noses happily with Timmy.

"Do seals *like* fresh-water fountains?" Jo asked Allie.

Allie shrugged. "This one seems to," she laughed. "Come on, let's get it some fish from the fridge . . ."

They jumped up and headed back into the living room. The ski-masked figure looked round, startled.

"Hey!" Jo gasped, stopping in her tracks. "Who are you?"

The intruder wasted no time offering an answer. She sprinted for the front door. Timmy jumped into her path with a ferocious snarl. She backed away, climbed over the sofa and knocked a pile of magazines off the coffee table in her haste to get away.

"Hey, my fashion magazines!" said Allie hotly, trying to grab the woman as she raced past. "I had those arranged by season!"

The woman reached the patio doors. She sprinted through them, past the fountain. To her astonishment, a seal popped its head out of the fountain and barked at her. Caught by surprise, she staggered backwards and stepped in the fountain by mistake. Righting herself, she ran on through the patio and down to the beach.

The Kirrins ran out of the patio doors. The masked figure had already reached the shore. She shoved a hapless man off a jet-ski, leaped aboard and powered out into the ocean.

"Comes into our house, makes a mess, doesn't say goodbye," Dylan muttered, as they watched the mystery figure make her escape. "Whatever happened to manners?"

Chapter Three

As they turned back to the house to see if anything had been taken, Timmy started barking. He had noticed something in the sand near the patio. Walking over to where Timmy was standing, Max studied a footprint the intruder had left in the sand.

"Hey, look what Timmy found," he called over to the others as they made their way over. "There's a picture in the bootprint . . ."

Jo ruffled Timmy's black and tan neck with pride. "Good job, Timmy," she said.

Allie had found another print a stride further on. "This has a picture, too – it's the Scrappy Flapjacks' logo," she said. "The boots must be from Cowboy

Town. Maybe Mr Ski Mask works there."

Jo left the beach and headed back to the patio door. "There are grease smudges all over the door . . ." she said, examining the glass. "Ski Mask could be a ride operator – that would get his hands greasy."

Allie pulled out her sparkly pink mobile. "I'll report what we know to the Sheriff's office – they can sniff around Scrappy's," she said, dialling and then pressing speakerphone.

"This is the Sheriff's Office," said a chirpy automated voice. "Our operators are busy. Estimated hold time is . . . fourteen hours six minutes and ten seconds."

A burst of muzak followed this announcement. Allie gazed at the others. "Or we can go to Scrappy's ourselves . . ." she suggested.

The Five headed back to Scrappy Flapjacks' the following day, determined to identify the ski-masked figure that had broken into the beach house. Their rucksacks were stuffed with the usual things you might need on a day out: torches, matches, compasses.

Jo pulled a folding map of the park out of her pocket.

"The steam train is the only mechanical ride here," she said, studying the map. "It stops at Rattlesnake Gulch, Scorpion Flats and Bleached Skull Junction."

She handed the map to Dylan, for him to tuck into her overloaded rucksack. Trying to find somewhere for the map to go, Dylan pulled out an assortment of objects, including the ceramic cactus Jo had won the day before.

"Here's a tip, Jo," said Dylan, waving the cactus around. "If you unpack your rucksack at the end of every day, you won't have so much junk in it."

As he put the cactus back, a little steam train came tootling round the corner and stopped at the small Old West train platform in front of them. There was a whoosh of steam. The Five waited eagerly for the train driver to show himself.

"Mr Ski Mask was about medium height and weight . . ." Max began.

The door to the tiny engine cab opened. An impossibly tall, heavy man unfolded himself from the seat and stood up.

". . . and that man is a giant," Max concluded faintly.

"Tickets, please!" the engineer said in a deep bass voice. "All aboard!"

Allie approached him. "Excuse me, Mr Engineer," she said politely. "Would you by any chance know someone who works here who gets their hands greasy?"

The engineer grinned. "Try the cook at the park café," he said. "He makes the greasiest food in the world! Ha-ha!" He stopped chortling. "Seriously," he advised, "don't get the chilli-burger – it's a gut bomb."

And he folded himself back into the tiny engine cab and started up the train again.

As the steam engine whistled off into the distance, the Five walked back down into the heart of the cowboy town.

"So, which way is the café?" Max said. His stomach had started rumbling.

"Max," Jo warned, "food grease isn't what we're looking for."

They wandered past the bank and the county jail. Then they passed a souvenir cart, selling

bottles of dark brown liquid.

"Hey, Max, if you're hungry, I dare you to eat this –" said Dylan, plucking one of the bottles off the cart. *"Scrappy's Jalapeno Tonguefire Sauce."* He waggled his eyebrows at Max challengingly. "Think you can handle the heat, tough guy?"

"I can handle anything you can handle, Iron Stomach Man," said Max at once.

Without a word, Dylan handed the cart attendant some cash. Each boy took a cracker from a basket on the cart counter. Dylan splashed a little sauce on each cracker.

"Choose your weapon . . ." he said, offering the crackers to Max.

The boys started staring each other down like they were in an old cowboy film. They narrowed their eyes. They flexed their fingers.

"Ready . . ." said Max. "Set ... chomp."

Allie and Jo watched with amusement as Max and Dylan both put their crackers in their mouths and chewed.

"That's not so—" Dylan started pleasantly. Then . . . "BWAAAAAGGGHHHHH!"

"FWUHHHHHHHHH!" Max added.

They fanned their mouths as their faces turned purple. Steam shot out of their ears and they hopped up and down uncontrollably.

"Woohhhh!" screamed Dylan.

"Ahhhhhhh!" shrieked Max.

They both raced to a nearby water trough. Shoving aside the plastic horse which stood at the trough, they plunged their heads into the water.

"Some days they're very clever," Jo observed. Steam was somehow still rising through the water in the trough. "Some days, not so much."

A grizzled, grey-haired, wild-eyed apparition came hurrying down the street towards them. A battered old hat sat on the back of his head, and he was dressed like a threadbare gold prospector. Jo was reminded irresistibly of Al Fresco Freddy, the local eccentric character back home in Falcongate.

"Tarnation!" wheezed the apparition happily. "Looks like someone tried some of Scrappy's Tonguefire Sauce! Jeee-hosephat!"

"Wow – you're Scrappy Flapjacks himself!" Allie gasped.

Chapter Four

Scrappy Flapjacks thumbed his hat at Allie and Jo. "In the genu-ine, hardscrabble mule-headed flesh!" he said with a little bow. "Hooo-eeeey!"

"Mr Flapjacks," said Jo eagerly as Max and Dylan emerged from the trough. "My cousins and I are trying to get some information about a crime."

Scrappy's crazy white eyebrows started jigging around his face. "Someone hold up the stagecoach?!" he cried. "Let's get up a posse! We'll need cornbread 'n' beans!"

"You don't understand," Dylan put in as the old man wheezed with laughter. "Someone broke into our house. We're trying to find out who and why."

Scrappy slapped his knee and hooted. "Maybe the Dawson Gang did it! They're the dag-nabbedest desperados who ever scratched an itch!" He suddenly pointed over the Five's heads. "Hey, it's Sammy Sombrero!"

The Five spun round in surprise. A plush, six-foot tall sombrero was heading their way, its goofy foam face grinning at them.

"Somebody else can interrogate Sammy," said Jo a little weakly. "I don't speak 'hat'."

There was something mesmerising about the way the enormous foam sombrero bobbed and waved down the street towards them. Which meant no one was expecting it when the sombrero reached out a skinny arm, dived into Jo's rucksack, grabbed the ceramic cactus and fled.

"Hey!" Max gasped. "The sombrero stole Jo's cactus!"

Jo, Allie and Dylan had already started running after the foam-rubber thief.

"There's something I never really say back in England," Max muttered, shaking his head and taking off after the others.

Sammy the Sombrero had a good head start.

He'd already made it to the steam train, which had stopped in the station again. Scrambling to the top of the guard's van as the train tootled and threw up great clouds of steam, he started running along the roofs of the train carriages. Undeterred, the Five followed.

As Sammy reached the front carriage of the train, the roof gave way. The giant hat fell through with a yell. Recovering before the Five could jump down on top of him, he flung open the door of the carriage, ran off the station platform and disappeared towards the Gold Mine. The Five leaped off the top of the train, still giving chase.

The Gold Mine consisted of a long, wooden sluice like a half-drainpipe with water running through it. The sluice ran down a gully towards a small fake mountain. Streams of water gushed down the mountain, adding its power to the rushing sluice. Rocks, stones and pebbles were washed along, supposedly shedding their gold as they went. Dylan kept stopping and picking up the rocks, muttering a little feverishly about gold, and losing concentration. The hat was getting away.

"Not gold . . . Not gold . . ." Dylan stumbled and nearly crashed into Allie, running a little way ahead of him, as he stooped and checked, checked and stooped. "Somebody's teeth braces – ick!"

Sammy the Sombrero had reached the bottom of the fake mountain. He started climbing. Scrappy Flapjacks came dashing up, twirling a lasso over his head as the Five started up the mountain after the cactus thief.

Suddenly, the top of Sammy's sombrero snagged on an overhanging tree branch. The hat ground to a halt, struggling to free itself.

"He's stuck!" Jo yelled, picking up speed as she clambered up the mountain with the others close behind. "Grab him!"

Scrappy chose the moment to let go of his lasso. It whipped through the air towards Sammy – but fell short, catching the Kirrins instead. The cousins were brought to a complete halt, their arms pinned to their sides.

"Hey!" Jo yelled, struggling uselessly.

"Woahh!" roared the others. "What? Aargghh!"

"Dag-doodle the tar-flap!" shouted Scrappy, hopping around in agitation as he tried to free the

Five. "Sorry there, pardners, I was aiming for the hat!"

Speaking of hats, Sammy the Sombrero had unhooked himself from the branch. Now he ran over the top of the fake mountain and vanished from sight.

"Too late," Dylan sighed, struggling to free himself from the binding rope. "The sombrero's gone *adios*."

Chapter Five

Rather sheepishly, Scrappy removed the lasso from round the Five.

"If I ain't the clod-brained-est stew-head that ever wore long-johns!" he apologised, taking off his hat and scratching his wild white head. "I let him get away!"

"But we know we're looking for a giant sombrero-man," Allie soothed, stepping away from the rope. "He'll kind of stand out in a police line-up."

Scrappy looked even more apologetic. "'Fraid not," he said. "I came across the *hombre* who plays the Sombrero back a-piece. All trussed up. Varmint

conked him and took his hat-suit."

The cousins looked at the old man blankly, wondering what he'd just said.

"I think that means the bad guy took the Sombrero costume for a disguise," Allie translated at last.

Scrappy gave a wretched nod.

"Sorry, Jo," said Dylan. He patted her on the shoulder. "I think your ceramic cactus is gone for good."

"And it's all my dad-burned fault!" Scrappy groaned, looking like he was about to burst into tears. "Least I can do is give you another one . . ."

Dusty, the woman in charge of the bow-and-arrow game booth, didn't seem surprised to see the Five back again. Wordlessly, she handed Scrappy a replacement cactus. The old timer handed it to Jo.

"There ya go, little cowgirl," he said as he pressed it into her hands. "Good as new."

Jo looked at the new cactus. "Thanks," she said. "It's weird," she added, almost to herself. "It's just a cheap souvenir, but someone went to an awful lot of trouble to steal it."

"I bet it was the same person who broke into the house," Max agreed.

"It's only worth a couple of bucks," said Dusty disbelievingly. "Not really worth breaking into a beach house for."

"But still, a mighty pretty fake cactus!" said Allie brightly.

The others looked at her. What was with the jolly voice?

"Well, thanks," Allie chirruped on. "C'mon, guys!" And she led the others away from Scrappy, Dusty and the game booth.

As soon as they were out of earshot, Allie swung round. "That woman's a crook," she hissed.

Dylan was shocked. "Allie," he began, "I know they rig these games so they're hard to win, but that doesn't make her a criminal."

Allie shook her head. "She knew we live in a *beach house*," she said. "We never said anything to her about a beach house."

Dylan paused. "OK," he said at last. "*That* might make her a criminal."

Max frowned, trying to work it out. "But she works in a game booth – how would she get

greasy hands?" he asked.

They all looked back towards the booth. Timmy growled softly.

It was the end of the day for the employees at Scrappy Flapjacks' Cowboy Town. People streamed out of the staff gate, heading for their cars.

Dusty was one of the last to leave. The Five watched from behind a convenient patch of shrubbery as she walked over to an old motorbike and climbed aboard. She started it. It wheezed to a smoky stop after a couple of seconds. Dusty climbed off again and started tinkering with the engine, getting grease all over her hands.

"Greasy hands!" Max whispered in triumph. "She's definitely our man! I mean 'woman'!"

Dusty had started the bike again. This time, the engine held. Hopping aboard, she roared off down the winding canyon road that led away from the theme park.

"Well," Jo observed, "our woman is getting away."

The Five ran helplessly out into the road to watch Dusty go. Allie, however, looked up at a

nearby hillside. "No, she's not," she said with a grin. "C'mon . . ."

She started running towards the hill, where a group of hang-gliders were busily launching their butterfly-bright wings into the bright Californian sun.

"That's the Malibu Hang-Gliding Club," Allie explained over her shoulder. They scrambled on up the rocky slope. "I'm friends with their president . . ."

The others didn't grasp what Allie was getting at until they found themselves being padded up,

helmeted and strapped into hang-gliders while Allie chatted to a young man with 'Malibu Hang-Gliding Club' embroidered on his fleece. As Timmy got strapped in to one of the hang-gliders beside Jo, Allie came over to join them, wriggling deftly into the hang-gliding harness as if she'd done it a hundred times before. Which she more or less had.

"How're you doing, Timmy?" Jo shouted over at Timmy as they all launched off from the top of the hill and soared into the sky.

Timmy barked happily.

The road below looked like a tiny ribbon. They spotted Dusty speeding along on her motorbike, throwing up little puffs of red dust as she went. Swooping down, the Five followed her along the road. When she reached a tunnel, they angled their gliders up and zoomed over the top of the mountain like they were on some huge airborne rollercoaster.

They found Dusty on the far side of the mountain. She had turned on to a private road and was motoring along towards a large complex of apartment buildings at the foot of the Malibu mountains.

Soaring over her head, the Five brought their hang-gliders down to land at the entrance to the complex. They unstrapped themselves quickly, and stowed the gliders and equipment in the undergrowth. Then they hid, watching as Dusty roared up to the front gate and stopped beside a keypad. She swiftly punched in a four-digit code. The gates swung open, and Dusty drove inside.

The Five scrambled to their feet. They dashed for the gate, but it had already swung shut. Jo tried it. It was locked.

"How are we going to get in?" Allie wailed.

The gate was unmanned, and well over two metres high.

Max smiled. "Same way *she* got in," he said. "We'll punch in the code."

"I don't know the code," Dylan said, shaking his head. "Allie, Jo, do you know the code?"

Max pointed at the keypad. "Only four of these keys have grease on them," he said. "The greasiest one is the one she pushed first . . ."

"And the grease wore off as she went along . . ." Jo went on, her eyes widening as she understood. "Which leaves us with . . . 1, 2, 0, 4 . . ."

Jo punched the keys. The gate buzzed, and then slid open noiselessly.

"See?" Max said as the others gave each other high-fives. "If she took the bus instead of having a dirty, polluting motorcycle, she'd have got away scot free!"

Chapter Six

The apartment complex was arranged around a central courtyard with a swimming pool. Moving cautiously across the courtyard, the Five spotted Dusty almost at once. She was in the kitchen of a ground-floor apartment, speaking on the phone. And the ceramic cactus was standing on the kitchen table.

Racing over to the window, the cousins ducked down. They strained to hear what Dusty was saying. But the double-glazing made it impossible. Instead, they watched through the glass as Dusty wrote something on a notepad and hung up the phone. Tearing the top sheet off the notepad and

stuffing it in her pocket, Dusty then picked up a magazine and settled down at the table. She wasn't going anywhere.

"We've got to get that cactus," Jo hissed. "We need a distraction."

Unaware that she was being watched, Dusty yawned and flicked through her magazine. It had been a successful day, in the end. The whole business with the hat . . . Well, she'd got the cactus back. That was the main thing.

The doorbell rang. Dusty had just reached her horoscope, and ignored the interruption. But when it rang again several times, she sighed, folded up the magazine and went to answer the door.

No one was there. Puzzled, Dusty looked left and right. Then she looked down. A portable lawn sprinkler stood at her feet. Nearby in the bushes, Jo turned on the hose.

"Waagh – sppppppp!" Dusty spluttered as the sprinkler soaked her from head to foot. "Oopphhh!"

Dylan had opened the kitchen window, and Allie was now working quickly. She had fed the long vacuum hose from the swimming pool filter through the window until it was touching

the cactus on the table.

"OK," Allie whispered over to Max at the pool filter switch. "Turn on the pool vacuum."

Max obediently switched the vacuum on. Immediately, the mouth of the vacuum hose clamped on to the cactus and held it tightly. Allie carefully pulled the hose back towards the window, bringing the cactus along with it.

Dylan had now got hold of the pool skimmer net. He put the replacement cactus Jo had been given by Scrappy Flapjacks into the net and poked it carefully through the window. Deftly, he emptied the net and set the replacement on the table. Then, for good measure, he scooped up the notepad Dusty had been writing on and whisked the pole back out through the window. Mission accomplished.

Round at the front, the water in the sprinkler stopped abruptly as Jo turned it off and sneaked back to join the others. Dusty opened her eyes and blinked the drops from her eyelashes. "Now I won't need a bath till the weekend," she said to herself, before turning and heading back inside.

* * *

Back at the beach house, the original ceramic cactus took pride of place on the patio table. A desk lamp had been angled so that it gave maximum light.

Jo and Allie were scrutinising the cactus carefully. Jo picked it up and held it in front of the desk lamp.

"Doesn't *look* unusual," she murmured, turning it round in the light.

Allie used her fingernail to scrape a little paint off the cactus. "Hmm, nothing special about the paint," she said after a moment.

Dylan and Max arrived. They were carrying a grocery bag. The seal in the fountain popped its whiskery head out and gazed hungrily as Dylan unpacked a fish from the bag.

"There you go, old boy," Dylan said, smiling as he tossed the fish over. "Nice raw fish."

The seal gobbled down the fish in a flash. Allie winced.

"I guess that's officially sushi," she said reluctantly, "but usually sushi's eyes don't stare back at me. It's kind of scary."

"You think *that's* scary?" said Max, grinning. "Check this out . . ." He produced a bottle of hot

sauce from the grocery bag and waved it around. "Aaggh," Max added mischievously, "it burns my eyes just to look at it!"

Dylan read the label on the bottle. *"Liquid Lava Habanero Skull Sauce,"* he said, and shrugged. "I can handle that."

"The man at the shop said it's the hottest sauce on the market," said Max, putting the bottle down on the table. "You can use it to dissolve rust on battleships."

"And, for some reason, you two are going to eat it," Jo said.

"I'm going to eat it," Max said promptly. "Dylan's going to wimp out."

Dylan rose to the bait like a fish to a fly. "I don't know the meaning of 'wimp out'," he said at once. He produced a jalapeno chilli pepper from somewhere and waved it at Max. "Pepper . . . ?" he inquired.

Max held up his own jalapeno. "Pepper."

The girls stared open-mouthed as Max sprinkled sauce on his and Dylan's peppers.

"Don't watch this, Timmy," Jo advised, starting to laugh. "I don't want you to lose respect for Max and Dylan."

The boys popped the peppers into their mouths. There was a moment of silence. Then . . .

"MISTAKE!" roared Dylan. "BIG MISTAKE!"

Both the boys' faces turned a blazing shade of scarlet.

"You win!" Max choked. His eyes were streaming so much that tears were running down his neck. "Where's the hose?!"

He raced to the garden hose against the wall and turned it on.

"No, you win!" Dylan screamed, wrestling Max for control of the hose. "*I* get the hose!"

"You know," said Allie as the boys tumbled and rolled over each other in desperation, "water doesn't actually help with pepper sauce."

The hose had had enough. It split in half, water gushing out of one end and straight into Allie's face.

"And that *really* doesn't help," Allie added, spluttering and backing away. "Whooah!"

She tripped over a bench and fell into a hanging basket. The basket swung towards a shelf of decorative ornaments, knocking the shelf off its brackets and dumping the contents on to the ground. Timmy and the seal started barking like crazy.

* * *

"All right!" Jo yelled, trying to bring the chaos under control. "ALL RIGHT!"

Timmy and the seal went quiet. Max and Dylan, their panting mouths still open for a drop of water, stopped struggling over the useless hose nozzle. Allie wiped water out of her face and tutted.

"The hot pepper contest is officially a tie," Jo said, lowering her arms. "Congratulations – you're both quite foolish."

Dylan and Max shook hands with quiet pride. Their dignity was intact, if you didn't count the spectacle they'd just made of themselves. Jo looked at the scattered ornaments, her eye resting on the broken figurine of a sea-captain. "Although you've given me an idea," she murmured, and turned back to the ceramic cactus on the table. "If there's nothing unusual *outside* the cactus, maybe there's something unusual *inside*."

Jo smashed the cactus wide open. Inside its broken remains, a shiny metal object about the size of a mobile phone glinted in the desk light.

Jo prised it out. "Now that's no ordinary souvenir ceramic cactus," she grinned, examining her find.

Dylan took a look. "Who knows?" he said, as he tried to work out what the glinting object was. "Maybe all the Scrappy Flapjacks' game prizes have precisely engineered, high-tech components in them."

Max peered at something printed on the back of the component. "Masterdon Tech . . ." he read.

"'Masterdon' eh?" Dylan said, starting towards the living room and his laptop. He raised his fist like a superhero. "To the internet . . . !"

Chapter Seven

It took Dylan approximately twenty seconds to find out about Masterdon.

"They're a high-tech company," he told the others, swinging back in his chair so they could see the logo on the laptop screen. "Factories all over the world."

Jo pointed at the screen. "What's that?"

Dylan looked more closely. "Masterdon Tech proudly introduces 'SomiNar'," he read aloud. He scanned the rest, then looked up. "It's a sonic pulse device . . . triggers the sleep centre in the brain."

"So, what – it puts people to sleep!?" Max said, in surprise.

Dylan nodded. "Irresistible, intense sleep for up to twelve hours," he read off the screen. He pointed at one of the featured gadgets. "There it is . . ."

The screen showed a shiny, high-tech device about the size of a shoebox. Dylan hit a button. The device appeared to break apart, each component shooting off to a separate section of the screen.

One of the components was small, shiny, and about the same size as a mobile phone.

"That's *this*!" Allie cried, holding up the object they'd found inside the ceramic cactus.

"But if you could put people to sleep," Max said, frowning with the effort of working it out, "you could knock out police and rob banks!"

"That's probably why the SomiNar is illegal in this country," Dylan said, pointing at the warning sign blinking on the screen beside the device.

Jo took the component from Allie and studied it carefully. "So someone's smuggling a SomiNar in pieces inside Scrappy Flapjacks' game prizes," she said.

"That's a lot of trouble to put people to sleep," said Allie. "My history teacher puts our class to sleep every day, with no help at all."

Much as Jo hated handing stuff over to the police, she could see that this was a biggie. "I'd say it's time to report this to the sheriff," she said reluctantly.

Allie pulled out her phone and made the call.

"This is the Sheriff's Office," said the automated voice. "Our operators are busy. Estimated hold time is eight hours, nine minutes, five seconds . . ."

Allie sighed, and closed her phone. "Well," she said with a shrug, "we're making progress . . ."

Max started pacing around the living room. "But in the meantime, we don't know what that Dusty woman plans to do with the device," he said.

Dylan smiled. "Actually, we might," he said calmly. "I've got the notepad she wrote on . . ." With a flourish, he pulled out Dusty's notepad.

Allie shook her head. Dylan could be a real dope. "But she took the paper she wrote on," she said as gently as she could.

"Yes," said Jo, realising what Dylan was getting at. "But she left the paper underneath . . ."

She took the pad from Dylan and laid it on the desk. Then she picked up a pencil and shaded over the notepad. On the page, a ghostly image of white

handwriting appeared on the smudgy black background. It was a perfect impression of the words Dusty had written on the sheet above.

"21215 Rodeo Drive," Max read. "Nine p.m."

If there was one thing Allie knew about, it was shops. "21215 Rodeo Drive? That's Charles Harold Jewellers," she said promptly.

Jo smiled. "Then that's where we're going to be waiting," she said.

Chapter Eight

It was nine p.m. in Rodeo Drive – the home of excessive spending in Beverly Hills, California. Designer shops lined the street, their window displays enough to make even Allie gasp. The street, usually jammed with expensive cars, was almost empty.

Right now, Allie was too busy to admire the shops. She was somewhere altogether smellier.

In a dark alley off the street, five dustbins stood lined up against a wall.

"Couldn't we have hidden inside something that doesn't smell so terrible?" said Max from inside one of the dustbins.

Allie sounded tearful. "Yeah," she gulped. "Like a big bottle of perfume?"

The third dustbin along started to shake violently. The metal lid clashed like a pair of cymbals.

"Dylan?" Jo hissed, from the next dustbin along. "What are you doing?"

"I've still got the bottle of Liquid Lava sauce in my pocket," Dylan panted. The dustbin gave another heave. "It must be leaking – it really *stings*."

He stopped hopping up and down abruptly at the sound of a motorbike. Dusty pulled into the alley and turned off her engine. As the Five peeked out from beneath their dustbin lids, they saw a car pull in to the alley behind her. It was *huge* – a convertible with a pair of bull horns mounted on the front. The Five held their breath as the convertible roof was lowered.

Scrappy Flapjacks climbed out of the car, all tidied up and in his smartest cowboy clothes. Silently, Dusty handed him the replacement ceramic cactus. With a smile, Scrappy hefted the little cactus in his hands and smashed it down on one of his car's bull horns.

"What the jiggity-jabber-jings?" Scrappy snarled, hunting through the pieces. "Where is the do-dab thing?"

Dusty looked shocked. "It's gotta be there," she gabbled, helping Scrappy to sort through the broken bits.

"It's *not* there!" Scrappy glared at Dusty. "It's not there like a snowman's not in a blacksmith's furnace. *That's* how much it's not there!"

Dusty put her hands to her face. "What do we do?" she gasped. "The jewellery show's going on right now."

Scrappy took a deep breath. "Don't get your grub in a bucket," he said. "The missing do-dab is the automatic timer, but we've got the rest of the gizmo . . ."

Reaching into the car, he produced something the Five instantly recognised from the internet. It was the SomiNar.

"We can't leave it inside and have it go off on a timer, but we can set 'er off the old-fashioned way," said Scrappy, polishing it lovingly on his waistcoat.

"But if we're in there with it, we'll go to sleep," Dusty pointed out.

Scrappy smiled. "That's why Providence made earplugs," he said. He tucked the SomiNar into a briefcase and snapped it shut. "C'mon," he ordered Dusty, heading out of the alley. "Saddle up."

The Five listened as Scrappy and Dusty's footsteps disappeared out of the alley and on to the brightly lit Rodeo Drive. Then they climbed out of their dustbins and followed.

Jo had to drag Allie away from the gorgeous window displays as they concentrated on keeping Dusty and Scrappy in their sights. At last, they saw the two villains reach their destination.

Charles Harold Jewellers was a prime example of Beverly Hills elegance. Floodlights criss-crossed the front, and the window displays sparkled brightly. A uniformed guard stood at the door.

"Howdy, buckaroo," said Scrappy, sauntering up with his briefcase and Dusty close behind. "We're here for the jewellery show."

The guard gave a little bow. "Ah, Mr Flapjacks, very good, Mr Flapjacks," he said, detaching the velvet rope that hung in front of the door and allowing Scrappy and Dusty to pass.

"They took the SomiNar inside," said Dylan, as

the Five observed from a carefully chosen shop doorway. "They're going to rob the place."

Allie looked worried. "Charles Harold is the most exclusive jeweller in Beverly Hills. How are we going to get in there?" she asked.

Jo looked down at Timmy pressing himself faithfully against her heels. "Where there's a Timmy," she said with a grin, "there's always a way . . ."

A few moments later, Timmy trotted over to the guard. He panted, whined and barked until he was sure the guard had noticed him. Then he trotted on round the corner.

Jo gave it a couple of minutes. Then she approached the guard, thinking the saddest thoughts she possibly could to make the tears come to her eyes.

"Mister! Mister!" she sniffed, choking back sobs. "My dog is lost! He ran away! What shall I do?"

The guard melted. "Don't worry, young lady – I think I know where he went," he said soothingly. "C'mon . . ."

Stepping away from the door, he led Jo in the direction Timmy had gone. With the coast clear, Allie, Max and Dylan scampered through the unguarded door and into the jewellery shop. They could hear Jo outside in the street.

"That's not my dog! Maybe he went inside?"

"Hey, wait –" the guard called. There was the sound of running footsteps, and Jo burst into the shop with Timmy.

By the time the guard had made it back to the shop, the Five had disappeared discreetly behind an assortment of potted palm trees. They could watch everything from here.

It was a sight to behold. The jeweller's had been set up for a fashion show. There was a catwalk with a curtain at the back end, to allow the models to parade the magnificent jewellery up and down. Dozens of Beverly Hills millionaires watched the spectacle, sipping champagne from crystal glasses.

Scrappy and Dusty had shouldered their way through the crowd. Now they were approaching the catwalk. It was time for the Five to make their big entrance – and hope for the best.

"Give it up, Scrappy!" Dylan shouted, as the cousins emerged from their hiding places. "We know what you're doing!"

Chapter Nine

Scrappy's eyebrows waggled in shock as he saw the Kirrins. "Dusty, it's them varmints!" he screeched. "Turn on the sleep-a-ma-jig! Turn it on, flab-dab it!"

Dusty opened the briefcase and flipped a switch on the SomiNar. A low, throbbing pulse thrummed through the room. The models and the millionaires instantly sank to the floor, fast asleep.

The Kirrins tried to get to Scrappy, but it looked as if the SomiNar was too much. One by one, they fell to the floor and started snoring. Max staggered theatrically. Allie struggled too, before falling to the ground.

"Must . . . stay . . . awake . . ." Max whispered,

crawling towards a large buffet table groaning with food. He pulled himself to his feet and swayed, staring at an enormous bowl of mayonnaise. "Salad dressing . . . ooh . . ." he mumbled, and collapsed head first into the bowl.

Scrappy and Dusty stared around at the silent room. Satisfied that everyone was asleep, Dusty switched off the SomiNar. They both removed their earplugs. Then they started moving around the shop, scooping up the glittering gems and shining gold and thrusting it all into bags. Scrappy emptied the cash register.

"I want the diamonds!" Dusty said happily, running the sparklers through her fingers. "Ooh, and the rubies! I want 'em all!"

"Cash is mighty pretty, too!" Scrappy crooned. He folded the money into fat wads and stuck them in his pocket. "Crackly, crinkly cash!" He shut the till with a snap. "OK," he said, "let's vamoose."

They started dragging their booty to the door. The Five jumped to their feet, pulling out their own earplugs.

"Aha!" Allie said, delighted at the shock on the villains' faces.

"I'll say it again, Scrappy – give it up!" Dylan advised.

"Dad-rat it," snarled Scrappy as he realised. "Those kids had earplugs, too! They were playing possum! Skedaddle!"

As Dusty and Scrappy rushed for the door, Allie hurried over to a display counter. An enormous fake engagement ring stood on the counter. Allie picked it up and swung it experimentally. It was about the width of a plastic hula hoop.

"Good thing I'm a jewellery expert . . ." she said, and flung the giant ring through the air.

It landed on top of Scrappy and Dusty, pinioning them together.

"Dag-nab it – we've been lassoed!" Scrappy screamed as he struggled.

"I don't think you'll be needing those jewels . . ." said Max.

He took the bag from Scrappy. But Scrappy had one more trick up his sleeve. Slipping out of the giant ring, he seized Max around the neck. "Not so fast, sonny," he snarled. "C'mon, Dusty . . ."

Dusty took the bag of loot from Max's hands.

Then, using Max as a shield, she and Scrappy backed towards the door.

Thinking quickly, Dylan pulled the bottle of Liquid Lava sauce from his pocket. He crossed to an electric fan, which stood on a nearby counter. "Hey, Max," he yelled as he unscrewed the lid. "Liquid Lava, incoming!"

Dylan poured sauce into the whirring blades of the fan. Clouds of chilli pepper fumes wafted towards Scrappy and Dusty.

"Aggh!" Scrappy groaned, loosening his grip on Max and dropping the SomiNar. "My eyes are on fire! My lips are on fire. My whole heck-fire head's on fire!"

Still clinging tearily to the bag of loot, the villains staggered outside. The Five sprinted after them.

Somehow Scrappy and Dusty made it to the alley before Timmy could get his teeth into their trousers. They scrambled into Scrappy's convertible and sped away, with Dusty at the wheel. Undeterred, the Five hopped on their parked bikes and gave chase.

Chapter Ten

Dusty changed gear and headed for the coast. The blue ocean and the Santa Monica pier could just be seen. Scrappy had recovered from the Liquid Lava, and was issuing instructions.

"When we get to Pacific Coast Highway, we'll have a clear shot to Mexico," he said, rubbing the last few tears from his eyes. "*Olé!*"

The Five raced along on their bikes, still managing to keep Scrappy's car in sight.

"How are we going to stop them?" Max shouted. He stood up in the saddle to get more bite on his wheels.

"With good, old-fashioned technology," Dylan

shouted back. "Slow down a bit, Jo . . ."

Out in front as usual, Jo slowed her pedalling and allowed Dylan to catch up. Taking one hand off the handlebars, Dylan reached into Jo's rucksack and pulled out the SomiNar. Jo pulled the timer from her pocket and passed it to Allie, who fitted it into the SomiNar. An LED timer instantly lit up.

They were approaching Santa Monica now. Dusty and Scrappy's headlights were getting further away.

"Twenty seconds ought to do it . . ." Dylan panted. He set the timer on '20' and activated it. Immediately the numbers started counting down.

19 . . . 18 . . . 17 . . .

"Go, Jo!" Dylan yelled, and handed Jo the SomiNar.

Jo pedalled as hard as she could. The gap with Scrappy's car was closing. She gave an almighty heave, and flung the device.

The SomiNar flew through the air, slipped through the car's open window and landed safely on the back seat.

"That street there – turn left!" Scrappy shouted,

unaware of the SomiNar ticking down behind him.

"Turn left!"

3 . . . 2 . . . 1 . . .

The SomiNar clicked into operational mode, and started humming.

Scrappy yawned. "I said turb lrrm blmm blrrrrn . . ." he mumbled, before falling asleep against Dusty's shoulder. Dusty, too, dropped her head down to the steering wheel and started snoring loudly.

Unchecked, the convertible ploughed straight

ahead. Flying off the street, over the pavement and on to the pier, it rumbled along to the end and plunged off into the ocean.

The Five brought their bikes up with a screech and looked down into the water. Scrappy and Dusty bobbed in the waves, sleeping like babies. The tail-lights of the convertible could still just be seen through the dark waves as it sank quietly to the bottom.

Job done.

The cousins exchanged high-fives, and Jo found a couple of lifebelts, which she tossed down over the sleeping villains. Allie grabbed a nearby fishing rod and cast the line into the water.

"I hope I'm using the right bait for diamonds and emeralds . . ." she said, gritting her teeth as she started drawing in the taut line. The Five watched as the bag of jewels swung, dripping, on the end of the rod.

A police car screeched into view, its lights flashing.

"Good – the police can grab Scrappy," said Dylan. He imitated Scrappy's voice. "That polecat's going to the pokey till the next blue moon, jiggety-jab it!"

"Consarn it!" Jo cried, grinning.

"I'll be dagnapped!" yelled the others. "Flap-doodle! Jumpin' jeee-hosephat!"

Back at the beach house the following morning, the seal was still swimming about in the fountain.

"OK, little man," said Jo, shaking the bucket of fish she was holding. "It's really time for you to go back into the sea."

She started laying a fish trail across the patio and down to the beach. The seal followed, gobbling up the fish greedily.

"The fish are still staring at me," said Allie, starting to look a little ill as she and Dylan walked down the beach behind the seal. "From now on, I might stick to vegetable sushi."

They had reached the shore. "All right my friend, into the sea," said Dylan as Jo tipped the last of the fish into the waves. "If you find any sunken treasure, we'll split it fifty-fifty."

The seal stared at the water. It stuck in a flipper, then pulled it out quickly. It shook its head.

"What's the matter?" said Jo in surprise. "Don't you *want* to go into the ocean?"

The seal shook its head again. It gave a bark, reversed and waddled rapidly back up to the beach house, flopping up the veranda steps.

Inside, Max was in the bath. He took hold of a brush and started scrubbing his back vigorously with it. He was interrupted by the barking seal, which burst in and climbed joyfully into the tub.

"All right," Max spluttered as the seal kissed him. "You can come in. But I am not scrubbing your back . . ."

Epilogue

Scrappy Flapjacks' Cowboy Town was under new management and back in business. It was the perfect location for the Five to film their next Handy Hint.

As Dylan operated the videocamera, Max fiddled with a rope that had been tied into a loop. Allie stood next to him.

"Sticky Situation Number Four Hundred and Seventy-Three: You Have To Lasso Something," Dylan announced.

Max turned to face the camera. "Once you have a rope with a good loop in the end," he began, "start with a noose about half a metre wide."

Allie walked about three metres away from Max, who began to whirl the noose over his head.

"Twirl the noose over your head, from right to left, letting the noose slowly get bigger as you do," Max continued.

The noose began to expand over his head. Allie shut her eyes in anticipation of being lassoed.

"Step forward as you throw, with the right edge of the lasso a bit lower than the left edge . . ."

Max was so busy looking at the camera that he forgot to check his aim. The noose flew through the air, sailed harmlessly past Allie and settled over a vicious-looking potted cactus.

"Then just yank it on in . . ." Max told the camera.

Still not looking at what he'd caught, he gave the cactus a tug. It sailed towards him, spikes first.

Max yelled with pain. "But don't lasso anything with needles!" he shouted, plucking cactus needles out of his body. "Ow! Ow! Ow! Ow! Ow! . . ."

Alfie walked about three metres away from Max who sorted to admit the horse over his head.

Then the horse over Alfie's head, from right to left, letting the noose slowly get bigger as you did so [illegible]

The noose began to expand over his head, Alfie shut her eyes in anticipation of being lassoed.

Step forward as you throw, with the right edge of the lasso a bit lower than the left edge.

Max was so busy looking at the camera that he forgot to check his aim. The noose flew through the air and harmlessly past Alfie and settled over a [illegible] garden.

There was a [illegible] Max [illegible] told the camera.

[illegible] looking at a bunch of [illegible] because they [illegible] walked toward [illegible]

Max [illegible] with [illegible] But [illegible] anything with [illegible] "[illegible]" [illegible]

[illegible] "Oh! Oh! Oh!" [illegible]

CAN'T GET ENOUGH OF THE FAMOUS 5?

Then continue your adventure online to play games, meet the gang, learn cool tips and tricks, watch videos, grab downloads and more.

Check out www.famous5.co.uk **NOW!**